KIDS' LETTERS TO
TERRORISTS

A B S E N C E   O F   A N G E R

Edited and Compiled by
John Shuchart and Steve Scearcy

Personhood Press
"Books For All
That You Are!"
www.personhoodpress.com
personhoodpress@att.net
(800) 662-9662

Cover and Book Design by: Tracy Design Communications
Jan Tracy / Patrick Simon   www.tracydesign.com
Photography by: Steve Scearcy

PERSONHOOD PRESS
P.O. Box 1185
TORRANCE, CALIFORNIA

Personhood Press, P.O. Box 1185, Torrance, CA 90505

Telephone: (310) 514-2656
Fax: (310) 514-3155
Email: personhoodpress@att.net
www.personhoodpress.com

Printed in the United States of America

This book is dedicated to every child who deserves to be heard, but isn't.

Contents

Acknowledgements

Without a doubt, the heroes of this endeavor are the kids. We'd like to thank them for not just writing wonderful letters, but also for their help in creating our course, AFTER™, from which the letters in this book come. The incredible success of the course is directly related to their input, enthusiasm, and desire to help institute a curriculum that really excites students.

We'd also like to congratulate our partners, Ken Birenbaum, Izzy Denlow, Ron Fugate, John Meara, David Snyder, and Paul Vogel. They spend seventy percent of their days thinking we're nuts; the other thirty percent wondering what to do about it.

None of this would have happened without the support of Dr. Marjorie Kaplan, Superintendent of the Shawnee Mission Kansas School District, and Mr. Bart Altenbernd, Assistant Principal of Westridge Middle School. Dr. Kaplan immediately saw the educational benefits of the program and endorsed its use, and Mr. Altenbernd's enthusiastic support and management of the school's staff assured the program's success.

Finally, to our families: Stevie, Scott, Carrie, Missy, Nate, Charlie, and Zac. Thank you all for not having us committed. Yet.

Introduction

This book is the outgrowth of AFTER™, an interactive course on violence and terrorism we created for young teens. The course is conducted over three class periods and each session takes about forty minutes. During the final session, each student writes an anonymous letter to an imaginary terrorist.

After showing some of the letters to friends and relatives, we realized something truly remarkable; there was, peculiarly, in almost all of them, an absence of anger. Some were funny ("Why don't you come over here and teach the boy scouts how to live in caves?"), many were sad ("I just don't understand why you do what you do...don't you realize how hurtful you are?"), but almost all showed empathy and hope. A typical letter questions the terrorist's actions, but encourages future behavior ("Why do you think you have to do these things? You could become a doctor or lawyer.").

As parents, we shouldn't be totally surprised. After all, isn't this what we've taught our children? That people deserve a second chance; that people can change; that we should forgive others and encourage them to improve? It's hard to believe, but maybe, just maybe our young people are listening to us. At least some of the time!

As authors and editors, we've learned to listen, too. We've learned to listen to our kids. They have lots to say.

And they make sense. For instance, one of the students who took the AFTER™ course told us that terrorism and violence didn't start for her on September 11, 2001. She said it began for her a few years ago. She said she's felt terrorism firsthand, on the playground, from a bully who tormented her every time she had recess. She told us people needed to start treating each other nicer, and if they did, things like September 11th would never happen.

Another student told us that he liked writing the letter to a terrorist, because it helped him better understand how he really felt about terrorism. He said he thought most adults should write a letter, too. We smiled and told him to go write his own book!

We know you'll enjoy this book, but we also hope you think seriously about what the kids are saying. In many ways, they're just like you when it comes to terrorism. They're scared. And uncertain. But, probably unlike you in that they have so much hope, even for the bad guys. They think we need to give everyone a second chance, and that everyone can change and improve.

The stuff dreams are made of...
Nice.

John Shuchart & Steve Scearcy

August 15, 2002

1

YOU NEED COUNSELING
... OR A JOB!

We have had others like you that killed because someone or something told them to. Some have said it was the voice of the devil. Some, like you, have said it was the voice of god. I can tell you that all you're hearing are the loose screws rolling around in your head. You need to see a shrink and drugs. Lots of drugs.

You must have a good reason. It must be logical. Well bro it don't add up. With you one and one is eleven. It may look right but it is not. You need to go back to school.

I could almost bet the U.S. would pay for terrorists therapy. Try to learn how to manage your anger. There are better options.

If something is bothering you, you should let your feelings out, but not by killing innocent people. You should talk to someone about your problem.

There are better ways to get these things you are striving for. Go to school and become a doctor, teacher, lawyer or engineer, do something! ...There is always hope for you if you decide that this is not what you want to do.

You have an anger problem. You are way too destructive. Calm down and think peaceful thoughts. Do peaceful things to get your point across and you will be a hero. You can change. We could help you if you wanted.

I think you are in major need of **HELP**! That is the only explanation to your stupid actions. Your parents didn't love you did they? I don't blame them! You are a looser. Get a job loooooser. Focus on something else.

Since you can't think for yourself and make the right decisions I'll have to do it for you. YOU NEED A JOB. And the only one I can think of for you is garbage handler... with out gloves... on a hot day....

I am curious to see what you accomplish with your life. You have caused destruction, caused loss of life. What is the difference between you and a mad man? You need a padded room where the only person you can hurt is yourself.

I want you to remember this word...J-O-B. That spells job and you need one to keep you out of trouble.

I think you are too involved with yourself! Please get help. You need it. Volunteer and help some people that are hungry or something. What is there to care about if you don't care about other people?

I think you are a mad man with low self-esteem. I want you to come out of the cave and surrender and let the war be over. You'll get help in prison.

I think you are a really smelly person who lives with pigs and eats their ** ***! Go get a job or go to jail.

Why the heck are you a terrorist? Does it bother you that you are killing innocent people because you are MAD? You need to stop and try not to be so ANGRY!! From, ME, not a terrorist.

You are a sick
minded perso[n]
You use you[r]
religion as a[n]

You are a sick-minded person. You use your religion as an excuse to kill innocent people. IT IS COMPLETELY AGAINST THE MUSLIM FAITH TO KILL OTHERS OR YOURSELF!! America as a nation is not against Muslims, and even if it were, it is wrong to assume every single person is against you just because they are American.

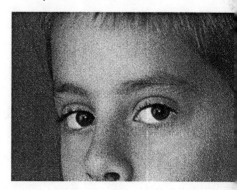

I feel sorry for you. You probably had a rough childhood, maybe with a lot of violence. With those problems you should go talk to someone. I want you to get help and change your mind. PLEASE. It would help the world.

Take some time and breathe. First you need to see a doctor. I think you might have depression. I think you need to talk and maybe need some medicine. You are sick but can get better.

You need to sweat. You need to pound rocks and yell and scream. You need to work really hard and get out your frustrations. Otherwise you could die of high blood pressure.

I have a video game with terrorists in it. They are the bad guys. It is a computer program. They have no choice. YOU DO! Get a job. Do something with your life.

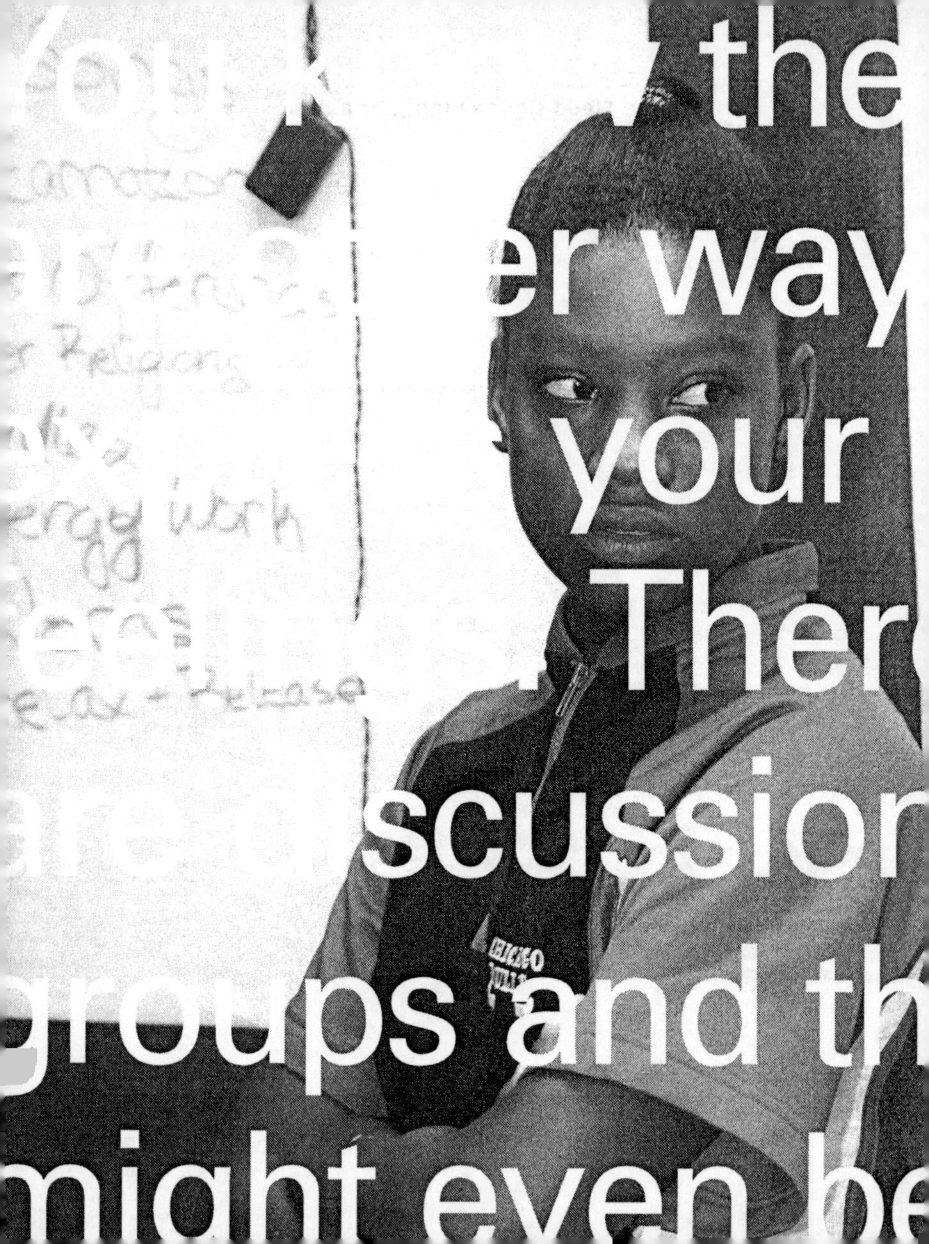

You know there are other ways to express your feelings. There are discussion groups and there might even be a CALM activist group. You could have gotten your point across in a different way. There are other ways.

We learned that people that do things like you do are usually loners with serious mental problems. You should not be alone. You should be with someone that really cares about you. And make sure you get mental help. Get help.

Everyone has been kind of quiet since you did what you did. They don't believe a person could do such a thing. This is not the kind of attention that will get you what you want. Climb a mountain or run a race or start a band. That will get you good attention.

You must be hearing voices. You must have ideas of being some sort of great person. I think that goes along with your illness. But maybe you are not ill but just full of hate. I would prefer you to be nuts. Get some help.

IF you have some emotional defect why handle it by killing people? There is a thing called a shrink! I want you— no, no—I force you to find a shrink and go for three months. And when you are not at the shrinks you must work with babies or old people every day. Let's talk after that. I think you won't be the same.

You have some serious problems buddy. You need to see a shrink. But I know that you won't go because you will be arrested. So send me your head and I'll see that it gets to the doctor.

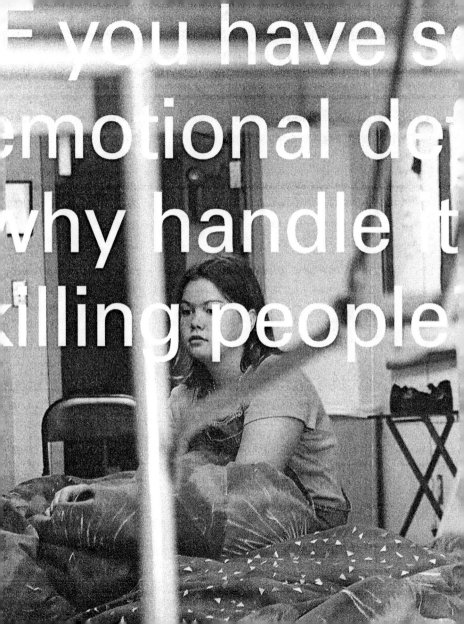

2

QUESTIONS:
WHY... HOW...?

Say you get to take over the U.S. , then what? What will you do next? Are you trained to run a country?

Now, sir, you are a terrorist. Why did ya become one? I mean did you just wake-up one morning and decide you were going to become one? Or did you go through a phase? Was your decision based on peer pressure?

You made it like it is permanently cloudy. It feels like there could be a storm at any moment. I guess this is what you wanted right? I live where there are tornados. And every year we live through that season. Why did you want to make another season to have to live through?

Why did you decide to become a terrorist? Was it the way you were treated as a child? Or was it because you wanted to be famous and powerful? Or was there some other reason? What ever it was I hope after receiving this letter you will change your mind about being a terrorist.

How could you do such a thing? You made me cry. You broke my heart. Your message was hate. But somehow in all of this my spirit grows hard and strong. You are so small...how can I expect you to answer my questions?

When we are young, we dream of being different people, such as athletes. Did you think you would grow up to be a person that kills others? Is this really the person you want to be?

I mean, why would you want to become a person who everyone is afraid of, or that everyone dislikes? I think that you, deep down inside, are afraid. You're afraid of people not accepting you for the real you, so you have to act big and bad.

What do you think you have accomplished by killing innocent people? Do you think your God (Allah) wants you to kill people, the creatures that he has made. You and your stupid punks think that you are the ones that decide who dies and who lives. Well I've got a news flash for you pal. That's NOT right. Think about it!

What in the world were you thinking? What did you think the outcome would be? It is never too late to take the high road. Please, you can think better.

All my friends are asking "why?" Not r understand

Why should we not consider you a monster? Why should we not consider you evil? I have heard that you call us devils.   We are not devils and perhaps you are not monsters but killing thousands of innocent people is what a criminal would do.

All my friends are asking "why?" Not me. I understand the rage you feel. I understand the hopelessness you feel. I understood it all on 9/11. I am in the 8th grade and understand you can not act on feelings of rage or live to promote hopelessness. I am a kid and know this, why don't you?

In the Bible and the Quoran too, killing is a sin. If your are so religious why are you doing something God does not approve of?

Why did you become a terrorist and what influenced you. Were you pressured by an adult or an older sibling??

Why are you a terrorist? There are so many other important occupations that you can do. Anything is better then following the rules of terrorism. So when you think about being a terrorist, think again.

There is smoke in my head. Things are unclear and I can't see. I do not know what to expect next. You have made us fear, for what? Are you really just a bully and nothing more? Did you know that a bully has no cause but himself. I think the same is true for you.

You are darkness. You are like something out of a bad sci-fi movie. A nameless faceless fear.

The ones you always kill are innocent. What is there about innocents that you like? Is it because it is easy? Is it because they are working to make productive lives and you just can't? Did the world steal your innocence and now everyone must suffer as you do? You are a mindless monster from some terrible story. But monsters in stories are interesting usually. You are not. You are just evil. And I wish you were not in my story.

I take it that you had some problems as a kid? If you did I'm sure that you weren't the worst off. Well all that I am going to say is that you made a stupid decision for your life.

Hello Mr. Terrorist, how are you? I bet you don't know who I am but I just want to know why you are a terrorist? Aren't you bothered that you are killing innocent people? It would bother me. What do you plan to accomplish in being a terrorist?

t is like hittin
aby bird wit
ock. You atta
he innocent,
suspecting
pe you see
ces of those

It is like hitting a baby bird with a rock. You attack the innocent, the unsuspecting. I hope you see the faces of those innocent, who like the baby bird did nothing but try to live a life. I hope you see nothing but their faces in your dreams.

I am a black female in the USA. I am 12 1/2 years old. You make things beyond people's control. Is that your plan to share your misery? Regardless I am not sharing. I am not buying into what you are selling.

If you think you are going to be more powerful by what you are doing now you are wrong. Now people think even worse of you. What are you thinking? I know you would be happier if you accepted other nationalities and religions.

I'd like to ask you some questions. Why did your dad and mother hate you? Who was mean to you? If you answer perhaps I can understand. I think you are really mean and a big bully.

Are you trying to accomplish something by killing people and bringing down buildings? Are you trying to be powerful? I want you to stop this violence and stop killing and make some good of yourself.

Personally, I am glad you are Islamic because that brings diversity to our nation. Killing in the name of your religion, what did you hope to accomplish? You hurt your faith and your family. You were misled. Wake up if you can.

56

diversity to o

nation. Killing

the name of

religion, wha

you hope to

accomplish?

urt your fait

Do you regret what you have done? I have done some things in my life that I regret. But nothing compared to what you have done. How can you feel good? How can you call yourself a hero? How can you believe that a god would require this of you?

Did you attack your enemy? Were the mothers your enemies? Were the fathers your enemies? Where the children your enemies? Or does it matter only to kill and draw attention to yourself? That is the real reason isn't it?

Are you some kind of adrenaline junky? A power freak? Or are you just mad? We have all lost something in this. Some have lost loved ones; some have lost a safe feeling.... you have lost control over what your life is about. Now it is all about this....hopeless.

I guess it could even happen in Kansas, now. Please don't come. Terrorism is not cool. Sincerely, your hated friend.

Hello, how are you? I am fine. Terrorists are terrible people. A terrorist like you murdered my aunt. You may think you are religious but you are not. I would ask you to do 3 things. One, come to America and see how we really are. Two, ask the president and go on national television and tell us why you do the things you do and how you feel about Americans. Three, leave America and tell the world how kind and caring the American people really are. Thank you for your time.

At my church we say, "God is where I am".
Can you say that?

What do you do for fun? Do you ever laugh? I can't believe that you do. Really. Just sitting around laughing with your friends. How could you? This is what you created for yourself.

Terrorism is madness. It is vicious and mindless.
It is easy. It gives the mindless a sense of purpose.

You have succeeded. If your goal was to make me afraid, I am.

Yes, I know you are fighting for a good cause but why kill people that have NOTHING to do with it. They were innocent. I am a Muslim too, and I don't go around killing innocent people to win! And guess what, you didn't make this better you made it worse. You are changing the rules to our religion. Does the Quoran say you should kill innocent people? You are a disgrace to our religion!

How could you truly know what you have done? How could you know the pain and anguish of all this. The destruction is your trophy but you cannot know truly what you have done.

ouse but wh
people that h
NOTHING to
with it. They
innocent. I ar

Who are you doing this for? I don't get it. There is no religion that would say for you to do this. What is your cause? We are against hunger and oppression; if these are your causes we are on the same team.

When you are alone, what do you hear and see? After what you did I would be afraid.

Did you look the people in the eye that
you killed? Did you look at the children?
Did their deaths make a positive effect
on the world? Did you explain that to them?
I doubt it.

3

OH YEAH! WELL...

Ok, get this and get it good. Terrorism is like whining. I am an expert at whining. Like my Mom says, it gets you nothing. I am here to tell you she is right. You don't get what you want and you spend a lot of time in your room. And since you live in a cave that wouldn't be good.

You're headed down the wrong road, buddy. Think for yourself and don't listen to your friends. What goes around comes around.

I don't know you, and I can't say I'd ever like to meet you, but I can say I really dislike you. I want you to go away and never come back.

I am very upset with you! Not only that but I'm embarrassed to even be around you. ...I want you to reconsider everything you are doing and stop living your life this way.

I want you to crawl down a hole and put snakes in your pants and never come out. Get a life you idiot.

Thank you for your time!

You are not making a point or making the U.S. weak. You've made us stronger! Congratulations on being Mister Big Fat Failure.

You took out a loan that is going to be painful to pay back. Check please!

I think you are a coward and selfish. You are afraid to actually fix your problems reasonably. You only care about you or your family's dignity! I think you should stop these acts of terror. They serve no purpose. I hope I have influenced you to stop this "business".

Sup yo Terrorist, What are you up to? I'm doing good. Hey I don't appreciate the whole terrorism thing. And about what I think of you, I hope you drop the soap in prison.

When you look in the mirror it really has to make you mad.

I am an Arab American and I hate you for what you have done. I hate you for hurting my country. I hate you for making me feel not so free. You suck.

We will rebuild. You won't. We will go on. You won't. I promise.

I want to talk to you out there, the ordinary terrorist. You are probably going to die and have a miserable life while some big dude becomes a hero and has an easy life. Think about it..sucker@#$%.

To me, terrorism is for wimps..

Come over here buddy and I'll show you some terrorism. You disgust me! You are ruining the world! Hello! Are you listening to me? Stop it NOW. Are you listening?

I hope you go to jail, and if you still don't feel bad...I hope you become someone's girlfriend.

What's ↑ homies? Why do you do what you do?? You don't have a real clue do you? I think you are a crazy mother. And not the kind that will get a card on Mother's Day. I want you to bug off.....

life, we're the
frickin' Unite
States of Am
By destroyin

That was the most stupid thing you could have ever done in your whole life, we're the frickin' United States of America. By destroying the twin towers, you made us open our biggest can of whoop ass you will ever see.

Stupid is as stupid does. What's up stupid?

I think terrorism is for dumb ***es. I think that you are a **************! Your name is a four letter word.

If I could, I would get you and put you to death for what you did. What do you think about that? Well thanks for your time. Peace.

Dear Retarded Terrorists, you are stupid. Why do you wear those turbans? Is it is a fashion statement? Well it's not working!

I think you should be placed on a secluded island and never allowed to come back. And all you would have to talk with would be your self and the ghosts of all the people that you killed. I think that would be good. Enjoy the beach.

Hey Buddy-boy, you really stink
Like something I wash down my sink
You're slimy and grimy
Cause you committed a big ol crimie.

Roses are red, violets are blue, terrorism sucks and so do you-butt face.

I hope you are hiding way down deep in your cave and the lights go out and you have no flashlight. Congratulations, you are now part of a landfill.

My whole family is frightened, even my dad. We had planned our vacation and you know what? We're still going. There will always be sickos like you.

Why in the world would you choose terrorist as an occupation? What do you hope to accomplish? Getting another star on your turban? I hate terrorist and the US hates you. Your face is on every milk carton. You know what I would like to do to you? I want to kick you and burn your turban. Well thanks 4 your time. In true Disgust, ...

So...you think you kill others and yourself and will go to heaven and be with 40 virgins?!?! My uncle is a drunk but even he knows this is crazy.

If you are killing people because they have more than you that's a stupid reason, and you haven't killed Bill Gates yet!

Your women are smarter than you. They cover their faces because they are embarrassed to be seen with you. And the same goes for the rest of us on this world.

I just have to tell you. You suck! That is basically all I have it say.

OK- you do a sneak attack, you kill innocent
people, destroy families, who are you?
(a) criminal _
(b) a terrorist _
(c) incredibly stupid _
(d) all of the above. X
That's right, an incredibly stupid criminal with
delusions of greatness.

You are sooooo stupid. You may have a legitimate cause but
no one will EVER hear you now. No one will ever believe you
now. The image of what you did is too big to ever forget. So
really, you are also a victim of your own incredible stupidity.

Hey congratulations, you're going to be remembered along with Attila the Hun, and Hitler. I'll bet your mother is proud. And I hope you have children that will ask you what you do.

The world is our sand box to play in.
And like my cat all you can do is poop in it.
My cat is not so smart. So stop.

I suggest something else to get attention...like a body piercing...with a telephone pole.

No country will claim you. You hide. You get the poor and uneducated excited with promises of wild greatness. You kill them for sure as you try to kill us. Do you have camel dung for brains?

Ok! You flat footed sand sucker. You would make a perfect ventriloquist's dummy.... speaking other's words and moving on their command.

So how long have you suffered from this terrorism disease? I have bad news for you. I think it ate your brain. Don't worry. Here's what you can do. Climb up in a tree and jump off headfirst. Twice. Then call me in the morning.

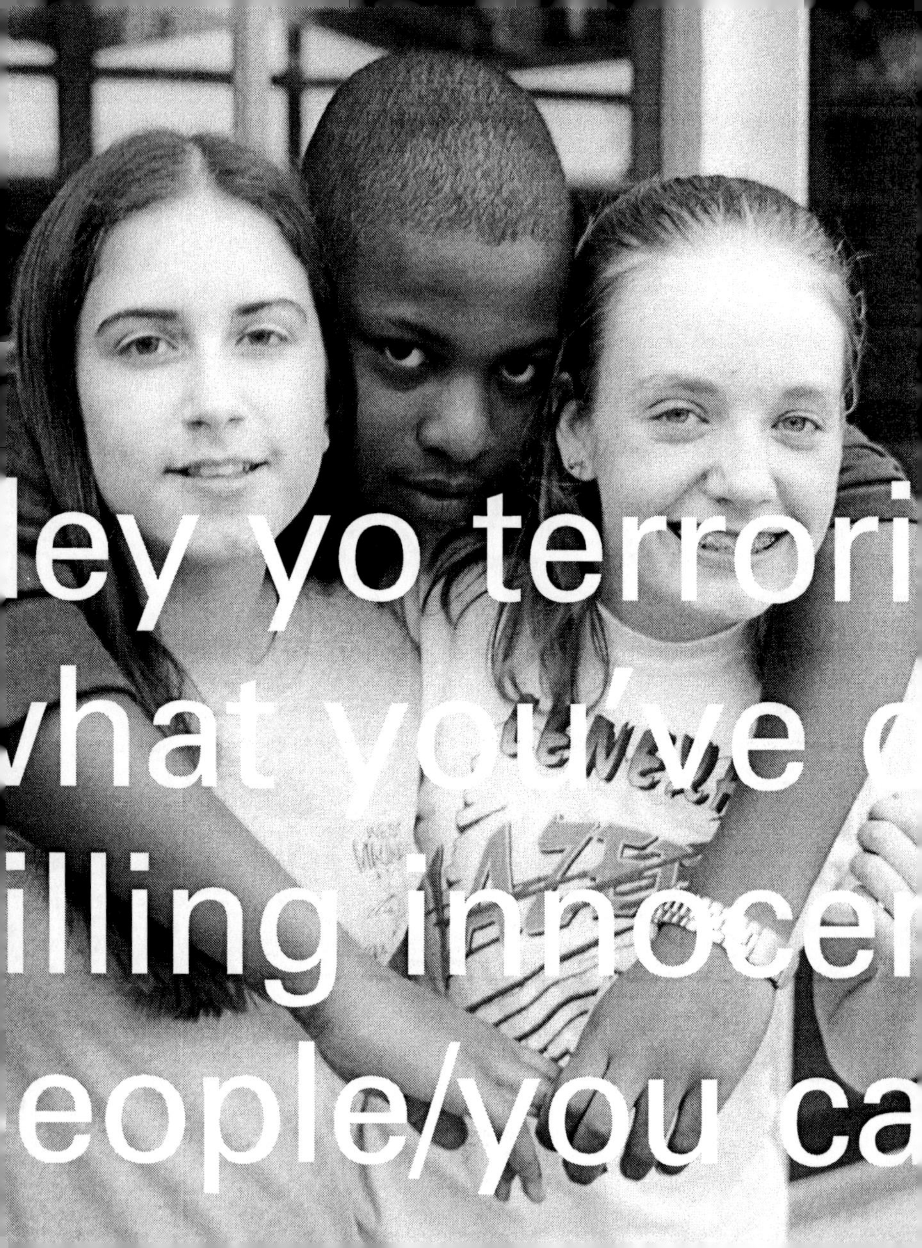
ley yo terrori
hat you've
illing innoce
eople/you ca

Rap:

Hey yo terrorist/look at what you've done/
killing innocent people/you call that fun?/
You call it clever?/you call it cool?/
you are one big big fool.//
You really stink/you live in a cave /
acting like that , WHO'S THE SLAVE?
Better think quick/
better think fast/
cause with us an enemy
you won't last. —Hey hey-ho!

The earth is too small a place for you and the rest of us to live on. We have studied various planets. May I suggest Uranus. You'll find your head there.

I know who you are! You wrote the book, <u>An Idiot's Guide To Really Stupid Things To Do</u>. You ought to know.

Well birdbrain you really dirtied your cage this time. And you're going to get plucked but good.

Well you made my list. My list of the three most annoying things in the world: you, athletes' foot, and warts. They are in order.

4

HEART AND
LOVING YOUR ENEMIES

I know you laughed and smiled when you did it. You thought you had hurt your enemy. You are wrong. I care for you even though you hurt us and laughed. I care for your children that are being taught to hate. I care for you that know only hate. You thought you had hurt an enemy. You are wrong.

.....But as I've grown I've learned that if there's a problem, the solution should never end up in violence....Do you think that life is only about revenge? If so, I no longer feel sorry for my country, I feel bad for you.

My grandpa says when we learn stuff sometimes it's like swallowing frogs.....big green slimy frogs. It is just hard to do. I want to hate you. But I am taught to forgive. You are the BIGGEST FROG I have ever seen.

I wish you would stop, change your life and start over. I think you should think about what you are doing.

Hello! How are you doing? ...When you were growing up didn't you have something you wanted to be like a fireman, or banker, something besides a terrorist. Why? Why did you have to become a terrorist? I want you to think about what you have done wrong and I want you to be ashamed you did that!

I hope you will never kill again. I hope you will find happiness. I hope there is peace for all of us.

You see holy war. We see evil terrorism. You have martyrs. We have victims. You destroy. We hope for the whole world.

Have you ever realized how in moments of anger and hate there are so many questions yet so few answers. These are times when we act on impulse and make mistakes. You made a mistake. Please consider your actions before you create more trouble for your self.

examine your
religious and
cultural beliefs
cover whet

I want you to strongly reflect upon my words about the lasting effects of terrorism. Examine your own religious and cultural beliefs to uncover whether or not they are really telling you that the right thing to do is kill humankind. My hope would be that you join others like me in praying for world peace.

I think you can do much better in life than scare people if you put your mind to it. If you work hard enough and try your best you can succeed. Don't be discouraged by failures. They help you on your path to success.

I look at people differently now. If I think they are from the mid-east I am afraid. I think they are going to hurt me. It is not right. Most of these people are very nice. But I can't quit the feeling of fear. I know I will get over it in time. But this must be how you live all the time. I feel very sorry for you.

Being a terrorist will not only hurt others lives it will also hurt your own. If you are trying to get attention, you are only getting negative attention. This will make people dislike you more. It would be better to try and make the world a better place for everyone. Than the attention you would get would be positive attention. Please consider how you would want to be treated before you act and do something that you can not undo.

You have your moment in history. Now you will probably get little more than that. You will not be worth remembering.

Please treat people the way you want to be treated. Your part of the world needs lots of help and we want to help. There are hungry people that need to be fed. Children that need schools. Stop what you are doing now so these people can get the help they need.

It is all such a waste. It is a waste of time and money. Nothing was accomplished. It is a waste of life. Who knows what those killed could have done. It is also a waste of you. What could you have done? Who could you have been?

You must feel so hopeless. That is the only reason I can think you would do such a thing. But please don't take your actions out on other people for what someone else has done to you in the past or the future. Look to the future for better things like family and friends. When you are at the bottom you can only go up. You are on the bottom.... My hope for you is hope.

What do you accomplish by doing these terrible acts? Please, before you ruin other's lives and even your own life, let's talk. I am sure we can work something out. Thank you for your time. Love, Someone.

You are a person just like me. I keep saying that to myself. You are a person that like me has made a mistake or two, got screwed up. I know that is the truth. If I don't remember that...I could become like you.

Even when I am playing soccer you are still in my mind. If I let it happen you are in my mind all the time. I will not let it happen.

You are a per
ust like me. I
keep saying t
o myself. Yo
a person that
ne has made

You boil it down and it is power isn't it. Power and not wanting to be the nothing that you are. It takes work to be something or do something. It is easy to do what you do. You want to really be somebody, bring peace to the world.

We studied your area. There is so much poverty and so many poor people. I can see why people have no hope. You exist because there is no hope and everybody is so poor. This is what you come from. It is so sad.

My country is a good country. My country has made mistakes but we never meant to kill innocent people. That is what you meant to do. A mistake is a mistake. If you mean to kill innocent people that is a crime.

I have a dream. I want to be a scientist. What are your dreams? What is it you want to be? I cannot guess what terrible dreams you must have.

I guess we have been lucky. Many parts of the world are attacked by your types. But we haven't been until now. It seems so strange. It seems like an old part of the world is attacking the new part of the world.

The babies of the world don't know what you have done. They are too young. I wish there was a way they would never know.

My parents say you are not new. They say there have always been people like you. This is news to me. I wish I did not know this. I wish you were not around me. .

I feel sorry for you. People may call you a hero today but tomorrow they will forget your name or be embarrassed by what you have done. It is only a matter of time.

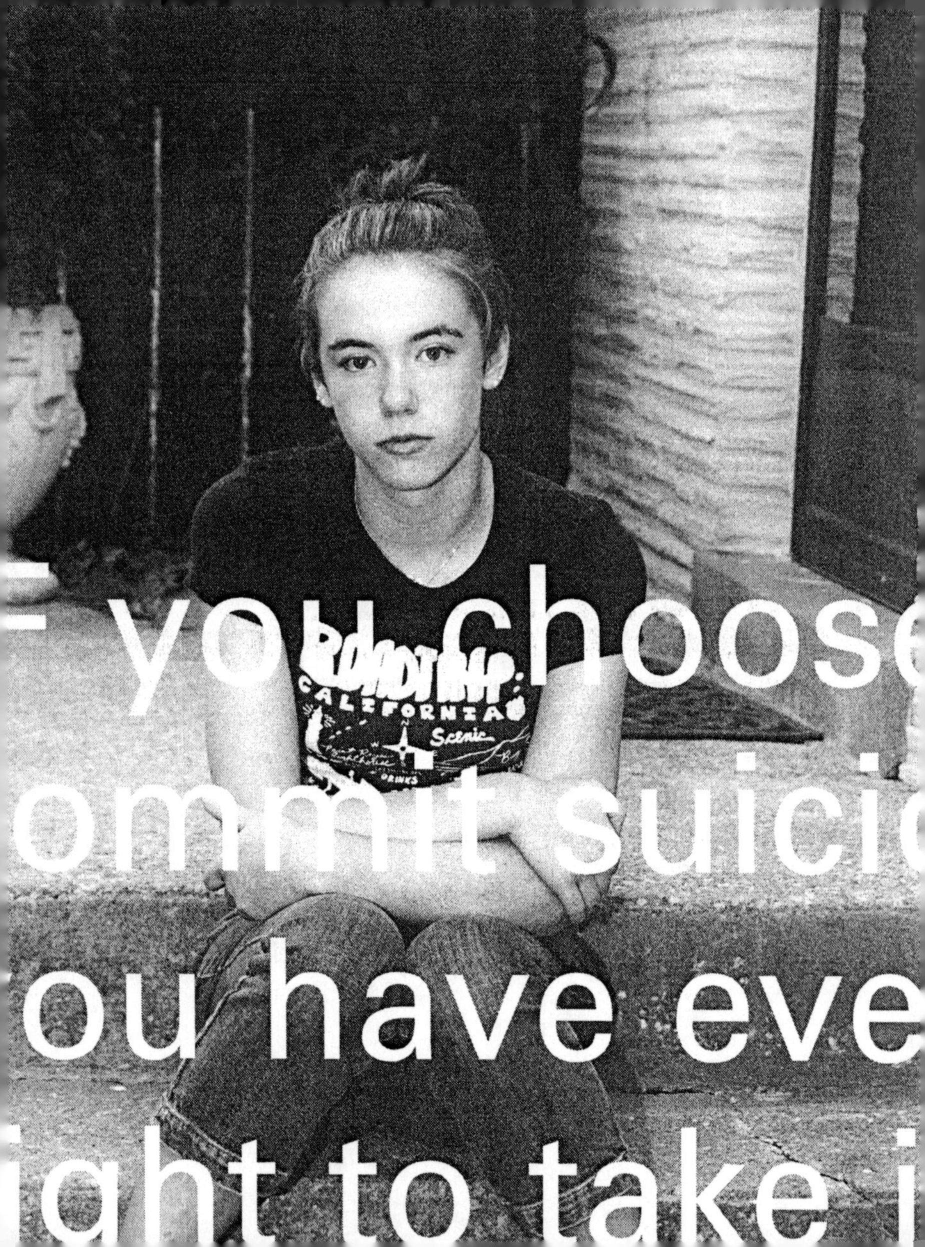

you choose
ommit suici
ou have eve
ight to take
CALIFORNIA
Scenic

If you choose to commit suicide you have every right to do it—but when you choose to kill innocent people while you are taking your life, that is not a heroic act. In fact I feel it is rather cowardly. I will not acknowledge or give any amount of respect for the choice you are making on behalf of your beliefs. Beliefs that have been corrupted with political ideals and goals. The real stuff of God is beyond such things.

What a sad hopeless view of the world you have. I guess that is why you do what you do. I wish I could give you hope.

You have made things different. And I don't like it. But I believe we can be better when this is over.

I hate you and I don't like that. I do not know the sound of your voice. I do not know your face but I hate you. I will take care of my hate. I will put it out. Please put your's out.

You are not a monster but you sure seem like it. You are a human just like me but it doesn't seem like it. We walk on the same world under the same sun and moon but I don't understand. Talk to me, write me back but please don't attack us.

If I saw you I would ask one question. What are you looking forward to tomorrow? And the next day? And the next? You see, I think you have no hope.

My mother cries a lot because of what you did. She is very sad. In a way you hurt our family. I hope we can get better and I hope you do too so this will not happen again. Violence is never the way. What you want to accomplish in no way makes what you did ok. With these sorts of actions you will never win..

My sister's best friend is from the mid-east. She says people look at her different now. She is a nice person. You are hurting a lot of Arab Americans.

I have two friends that are Muslim. They do not like what you have done. But we all feel funny when we are together. I hope you did not hurt our friendship.

I will pray for you.

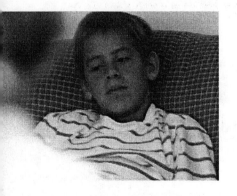

5
ADVICE TO TERRORISTS

"I think you should really reconsider the whole

terrorizing thing....."

You should do something positive with your life

and terrorism is a very NEGATIVE thing.

I think you should just give yourself up and turn
yourself in to the police.

*I think you should do yourself a favor
and take the elevator to the roof...walk
to the side and jump.*

....All you are is a coward and a follower. Step out of the box and think your own individual ideas! You need to quit being a follower and step up and become a leader. Be your own person! Do what is right!!

You may not want to listen to what I have to say. I can't tell you what to do. All I can ask of you is that you please rethink your actions.

Just visit our country and experience freedom. You'll never be a terrorist again. You'll never want to go back to the dirty place you live,......your mind. You can turn yourself around or turn yourself in or otherwise GOOD (us) is going to come down on BAD(you). And that will be the end of that!

Is your religion telling you to do this? Then maybe you should change religions. Do you think people don't care about you? Well they do care.....as long as you don't try to kill them. It is a good reason to stop.

f you have th
bility to get o
f terrorism y
hould get ou
ecause som

If you have the ability to get out of terrorism you should get out, because some day you will look back on this and not be happy.

I think I know why you are doing this? It's the heat. It is far too hot where you live,....may I suggest Antarctica.

Terrorism is bad. You should quit being a terrorist and get a job, start a family, and start over. Right now your life is dog doo doo.

It may be ok to kill people in your country but here in America it is just something we don't do. So my advice is that if you are still having those feelings look in the mirror.

Do something productive with your life. Become a Boy Scouts leader. You can teach the Boy Scouts how to live in caves. I'll write you another letter soon.

Terrorists...

Well, what have you done? Really? You killed thousands and made many times more sad. And the cause you helped was…..what? A religious one? A political one? It is not that clear. You hate Americans. That is clear. So because you hate you attack. GROW UP!

We build and have pride. You destroy and have pride. I want you to think a minute. Who is the real evil?

Yo bro...turban is way too tight. You are not seeing the world clearly. Loosen up and let the blood flow to your brain.

You wrap your violence in what you say is a noble cause. It is just violence. You are only fooling yourself. Study your history....the meanest and badest all had a noble cause.

You are slouchy, dirty and ugly. You need to see a psychologist or come and spend the night with a family that loves one another and then go back to your family.

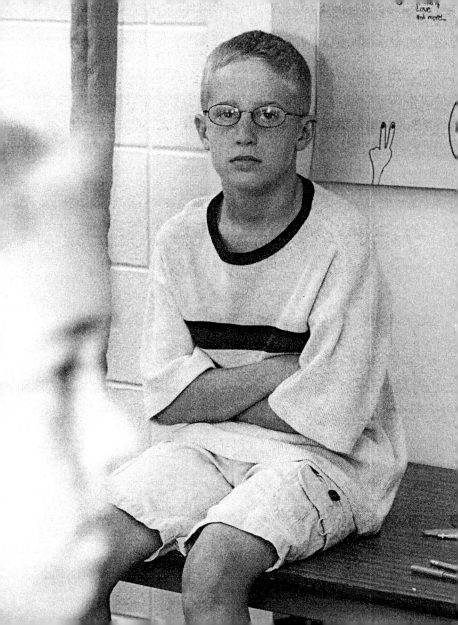

You've gotten some bad advice chump.
You're just going along because it makes
you feel good. Stop and think for yourself.

You have planted a violent seed. You will not like
the fruit. What you put out you get back.

This is not a game. This is your life. Don't blow it. You have talents in other areas. Find those and develop them and forget what you are doing now.

Trust me, there is no future in terrorism. There are no old terrorist walking around. There's your clue. They get killed. Hello...wake up! Stop this now. It is dangerous for all of us.

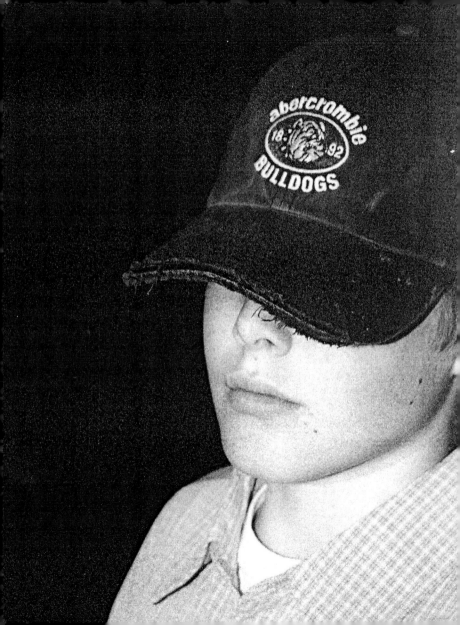

6

P.S. YOU ARE A LOSER!

P.S. I know you are going to read my letter and think rude thoughts......well rude right back at ya!

P.S. My brother is in the army and if anything happens to him &^%(^(%$^%$*$*&$*&^$. I hope we have an understanding.

P.S. There are two things that live in holes in the ground.... terrorists and rats. Hard to tell you apart.

P.S. You better treat your women better because a lot of them are probably smarter than you are. And from what I have seen of you men, you should have sacks on your heads.

P.S. From wh
can see a ter
s a lot like a
A mindless
weapon that
without thou
or conscienc

P.S. From what I can see a terrorist is a lot like a gun. A mindless weapon that kills without thought or conscience.

P.S. Thanks for reading my letter. Now I go home to a nice house and you crawl back to your cave. Is this the way you want your life?

P.S. At the end of the day what do you say to your family? Had a great day, killed 1000s. What's to eat?

Nanny Nanny boo boo-right back at you- Nanny Nanny boo boo boo -you're a pain on the kazoo.... I could just go on and on.

Concepts Simplified, Inc., "communicating life's challenging issues", is committed to working with young adults and their schools to create curriculum which motivates students to think, feel, and act upon the important issues they face. Our courses are created with direct student input and review. The result is a curriculum that not only achieves established objectives but produces motivated participation by students. Our courses are effective because we listen to the real customer. At Concepts Simplified, Inc., nothing gets done without the approval of the students!

Staffed by educators, business persons, and creative marketers, and aided by the students themselves, Concepts Simplified is making a difference in education by creating effective courses on Terrorism, Drug Abuse, Volunteerism, Conflict Resolution, Finance, Nutrition, and People With Special Needs.

For more information on our courses and how to get them into your schools, contact us at:

Concepts Simplified, Inc.
John Shuchart, President
11401 Brookwood
Leawood, KS 66211
(913) 485-3336
(913) 469-9737 (Fax)
jshuchart@aol.com
www.concepts-simplified.org
(website under construction)